MacMurtrey's Wall

Marc Sutherland

Harry N. Abrams, Inc., Publishers

L ong ago on a hill beside the sea, there lived a man who was tall as a tree, strong as a bull, and faster than the wind itself. That man was MacMurtrey, and he was greater than all men who had ever lived.

Late in the summer, when there was firewood to split and there were fields to tend, MacMurtrey would only swagger about, proclaiming:

"There are none so great, so great as me!"

All the while, MacMurtrey's people worked, doing their best to ignore his boasting.

But for all his strength and for all his skill, the great MacMurtrey was very unhappy.

Walking one day, MacMurtrey watched the birds and beasts moving among the hills and the trees.

MacMurtrey saw that these were very great things, and he grew angry. With thick, coarse hands, MacMurtrey captured every bird, caged every beast, and fenced in the hills and every tree upon them. When all these things were his very own, he declared:

"There are none so great, so great as me."

But still the great MacMurtrey was unhappy.

The next day, MacMurtrey sat and watched the blue sea. As the waves pounded upon the shore, MacMurtrey saw that the sea was very great indeed, and he grew angry.

"I will build a wall to cage the sea," he snarled. Then he would truly be the greatest in the land, and at last be happy.

And so MacMurtrey's wall began.

He cut down trees and tore stones from the hills. He brought a great ox to drag the trees from the hills, to the sea.

MacMurtrey worked in silence, from morning until night, with little food or rest. He sharpened the trees into stakes and pounded them into the sea to shape his wall's foundation.

MacMurtrey built great windmills to pump the sea away from the wall. When the ground grew dry enough, MacMurtrey set the heaviest stones.

Day after day, MacMurtrey set his stones while the sea, sun, and sky quietly watched. Slowly the green hills became barren and ugly in the shadow of the growing wall.

MacMurtrey's people could live in this sad land no longer. One starry night, they packed themselves and their winter stores in a boat and sailed away.

The great ox grew tired of the wall and the work that never ended.
One starry night, he, too, slipped away.

And all the while, the wall grew.

Then came the day when the wall was finished. As he admired his work, MacMurtrey roared:

"There are none so great, so great as me!"

He sat down to rest and waited to be happy. But the wait grew long, and happiness never came.

So MacMurtrey sat, cold and alone among the empty hills, until he felt the chill of a great black storm rising in the north. Soon the waves swirled and grew tall as mountains, and they crashed upon MacMurtrey's wall.

The great wall shivered and cracked.
Lightning splintered the sky.
Thunder rumbled and boomed and when morning came
the great wall was no more.

His strength gone, MacMurtrey could only watch as the waves washed over the remains of his broken wall. The falling snow and breaking waves lulled him into a deep sleep. Beneath the snow, MacMurtrey dreamed of days before the wall, when his people laughed and the hills were green.

Far away, the very storm that had felled MacMurtrey's wall blew his people off their course. In time, the sea returned them to the place they had left behind. Tired of being tossed about and longing for home and solid ground, they came ashore. There they found the ruins of a great wall and MacMurtrey sickly and asleep beneath the snow.

MacMurtrey's people built a fire and warmed his bones, fed him boiled oats, and wrapped him in blankets of wool. When MacMurtrey was well enough, the people said as one:

"We've cleaned your mess and kept you fed, now rise and help and earn your keep!"

Grumbling, MacMurtrey rose to help for the first time in all his days.

While the sea and sky sent wind and rain, and while the sun sent its warmth, MacMurtrey helped haul the remains of his broken wall away. He cracked stones to build cottages. He split wood for the hearth. He caught fish in heavy nets. He hoed the hills into furrows while his people planted seeds, one by one. Every day, MacMurtrey used his strength to help, as best he could.

At harvest time, MacMurtrey had grown strong again. The hills were full of good things to eat, and the sheep were thick with wool.

The summer's harvest was the greatest the people had ever seen. As they danced, the children sang:

"Old MacMurtrey, in all the land beside the sea, there are none so great, so great as thee."

MacMurtrey laughed, for he knew after all it was not so. But beside the sea, beneath the sky, under the warm sun, and among his friends, the great MacMurtrey was happy at last.

For Emily
Special thanks to Kayla & Taylor

Author's Note

I'm of Scottish and French descent, and the words and pictures in this story were influenced by
Norse mythology (hammers, ravens, storm gods) and Celtic folklore and art.
I studied medieval illuminated manuscripts and tapestries to understand how people from
long ago used things like the sun, birds, trees, and even giants like MacMurtrey to represent ideas.
I work outdoors as a land surveyor, near the coast of New Hampshire,
and many of the things I see during the day have also ended up in this book.

When I created the paintings, I first sketched out and did a tonal drawing with pastel pencil on illustration board.
Then I used acrylic paints to quickly add a wash of colors that dried instantly.
On top of this I added oil paints, because oil dries more slowly and is easier to mold or modify.
Finally I added oil washes to expose the colors underneath to give the illusion of depth.

Design: Becky Terhune

The art for this book was created with pastel
pencils and acrylic and oil paints on illustration board.

Library of Congress Cataloging-in-Publication Data

Sutherland, Marc [date]
MacMurtrey's wall / Marc Sutherland.
p. cm.
Summary: When strongman MacMurtrey attempts to show his power by
building a wall to hold back the sea, he learns that the power of
community is the greatest of all.
ISBN 0-8109-4494-4
[1. Parables. 2. Tall tales.] I. Title.
PZ7.S7272 Mac 2001
[E]--dc21
2001000631

Published in 2001 by Harry N. Abrams, Incorporated, New York
All rights reserved. No part of the contents of this book may
be reproduced without the written permission of the publisher.
Printed and bound in Hong Kong
10 9 8 7 6 5 4 3 2 1

Harry N. Abrams, Inc.
100 Fifth Avenue
New York, N.Y. 10011
www.abramsbooks.com